W9-DCL-406

09/2018

PALM BEACH COUNTY
LIBRARY SYSTEM
3650 Summit Boulevard
West Palm Beach, FL 33406-4198

Dear Parents:

Congratulations! Your child is taking the first steps on an exciting journey. The destination? Independent reading!

STEP INTO READING® will help your child get there. The program offers five steps to reading success. Each step includes fun stories and colorful art or photographs. In addition to original fiction and books with favorite characters, there are Step into Reading Non-Fiction Readers, Phonics Readers and Boxed Sets, Sticker Readers, and Comic Readers—a complete literacy program with something to interest every child.

Learning to Read, Step by Step!

Ready to Read Preschool–Kindergarten
• big type and easy words • rhyme and rhythm • picture clues
For children who know the alphabet and are eager to begin reading.

Reading with Help Preschool–Grade 1
• basic vocabulary • short sentences • simple stories
For children who recognize familiar words and sound out new words with help.

Reading on Your Own Grades 1–3
• engaging characters • easy-to-follow plots • popular topics
For children who are ready to read on their own.

Reading Paragraphs Grades 2–3
• challenging vocabulary • short paragraphs • exciting stories
For newly independent readers who read simple sentences with confidence.

Ready for Chapters Grades 2–4
• chapters • longer paragraphs • full-color art
For children who want to take the plunge into chapter books but still like colorful pictures.

STEP INTO READING® is designed to give every child a successful reading experience. The grade levels are only guides; children will progress through the steps at their own speed, developing confidence in their reading. The F&P Text Level on the back cover serves as another tool to help you choose the right book for your child.

Remember, a lifetime love of reading starts with a single step!

Featuring characters from *The Lorax* by Dr. Seuss, TM & copyright © by Dr. Seuss Enterprises, L.P. 1971, copyright renewed 1999.

Step into Reading, Random House, and the Random House colophon are registered trademarks of Penguin Random House LLC.

Visit us on the Web!
Seussville.com
StepIntoReading.com

Educators and librarians, for a variety of teaching tools, visit us at
RHTeachersLibrarians.com

Library of Congress Cataloging-in-Publication Data
Rabe, Tish.
Look for the Lorax / by Tish Rabe ; illustrated by Christopher Moroney and Jan Gerardi.
 p. cm. — (Step into reading. Step 1)
Summary: Easy-to-read, rhyming text introduces the Lorax and the place he calls home.
ISBN 978-0-375-86999-0 (trade) — ISBN 978-0-375-96999-7 (lib. bdg.)
[1. Stories in rhyme. 2. Imaginary creatures—Fiction.] I. Moroney, Christopher; Gerardi, Jan, ill.
II. Seuss, Dr. Lorax. III. Title.
PZ8.3.R1145 Loo 2012 [E]—dc22 2010050820

Printed in the United States of America
21 20 19 18 17 16 15 14

This book has been officially leveled by using the F&P Text Level Gradient™ Leveling System.

Look for
the LORAX

by Tish Rabe

illustrated by Christopher Moroney
and Jan Gerardi

Random House 🏠 New York

Blue sky.

Clouds fly.

Bright trees sway.

Cute suits!

Bar-ba-loots

play, play, play.

Bump, jump.

Jump, bump.

Run,

run,

run.

Hop, hop.

Flip, flop.

Fun,

fun,

fun.

The Lorax sees swans
swim, swim, swim.

The Lorax hears swans

sing to him.

Fruit sweet
to eat.
Yum, yum, yum.

Humming-Fish.

Happy fish.

Hum, hum, hum.

Big fish.

Little fish.

Swish, swish, swish.

High fish.

Low fish.

Splish, splash, splish!

24

The Lorax sees birds
fly on by.

Fast bird.

Slow bird.

Fly, fly, fly.

Bright day.

Light day.

Sky is clear.